16.95

Ft. Lupton Public & School Library

3 3455 02024 7760

425 South Denver Ave
Fort Lupton, CO 80621
303-857-7180
www.ftluptonlibrary.org

FORT LUPTON PUBLIC &
SCHOOL LIBRARY

FEB   '15

WITHDRAWN

D0461791

STAR WARS®
KNIGHT ERRANT
AFLAME

VOLUME THREE

SCRIPT
JOHN JACKSON MILLER

PENCILS
IVAN RODRIGUEZ

INKS
IVAN RODRIGUEZ
BELARDINO BRABO
MARCIO LOEZER

COLORS
MICHAEL ATIYEH

LETTERING
MICHAEL HEISLER

COVER ART
JOE QUINONES

As Jedi Knights, Gorlan Palladane and Vannar Treece long differed on what to do in Sith territory. Fearing for the safety of civilians, Gorlan abandoned the Jedi path years ago to lend assistance on his conquered homeworld of Chelloa. Vannar always preferred bold action—a preference that has proven disastrous.

Vannar's attempt to prevent Sith Lord Daiman from weaponizing Chelloa's vast stocks of deadly baradium resulted in death for him and his Jedi companions. All save one: young Kerra Holt. Finding Gorlan unwilling to rise against Daiman, Kerra takes it on herself to complete Vannar's mission.

But she discovers Daiman's brother and mortal enemy, Lord Odion, is preparing to move against Chelloa again. Fearing Odion's return with enough kinetic corruptors to destroy the planet's surface, Kerra launches herself toward the greater threat on what may well be a one-way mission . . .

This story takes place approximately 1,032 years BBY.

DARK HORSE COMICS

Spotlight

visit us at www.abdopublishing.com

Reinforced library bound edition published in 2012 by Spotlight,
a division of the ABDO Group, PO Box 398166, Minneapolis, MN 55439.
Spotlight produces high-quality reinforced library bound editions for schools and libraries.
Published by agreement with Dark Horse Comics, Inc., and Lucasfilm Ltd.

Printed in the United States of America, North Mankato, Minnesota.
102011
012012
♻ This book contains at least 10% recycled materials.

Star Wars: Knight Errant.
Star Wars © 2011 by Lucasfilm, Ltd. and TM. All rights reserved.
Used under authorization. Text and illustrations © 2011 by Lucasfilm, Ltd.
All other material © 2011 by Dark Horse Comics, Inc.

Dark Horse Books™ is a trademark of Dark Horse Comics, Inc. All rights reserved.
No portion of this publication may be reproduced or transmitted, in any form or by any
means, without the express written permission of the copyright holders. Names, characters,
places, and incidents featured in this publication are either the product of the author's
imagination or are used fictitiously. Any resemblance to actual persons (living or dead),
events, institutions, or locales, without satiric intent, is coincidental.

Library of Congress Cataloging-in-Publication Data

Miller, John Jackson.
  Star wars : knight errant. volume 1 Aflame / script, John Jackson Miller ; pencils, Federico
Dallocchio. -- Reinforced library bound ed.
     p. cm.
  "Dark Horse."
  "LucasFilm."
  Summary: Eighteen-year-old Kerra Holt, a Jedi Knight on her first mission, is left deep in
Sith space without any support or resources and realizes how unprepared she is, but will not
abandon the Jedi's mission to help the colony.
  ISBN 978-1-59961-986-6 (volume 1) -- ISBN 978-1-59961-987-3 (volume 2)
  ISBN 978-1-59961-988-0 (volume 3) -- ISBN 978-1-59961-989-7 (volume 4)
  ISBN 978-1-59961-990-3 (volume 5)
  1. Graphic novels. [1. Graphic novels. 2. Science fiction.] I. Dallocchio, Federico, ill. II. Title.
III. Title: Knight errant. IV. Title: Aflame.
  PZ7.7.M535St 2012
  741.5'973--dc23
                                    2011031240

All Spotlight books are reinforced library binding
and manufactured in the United States of America.

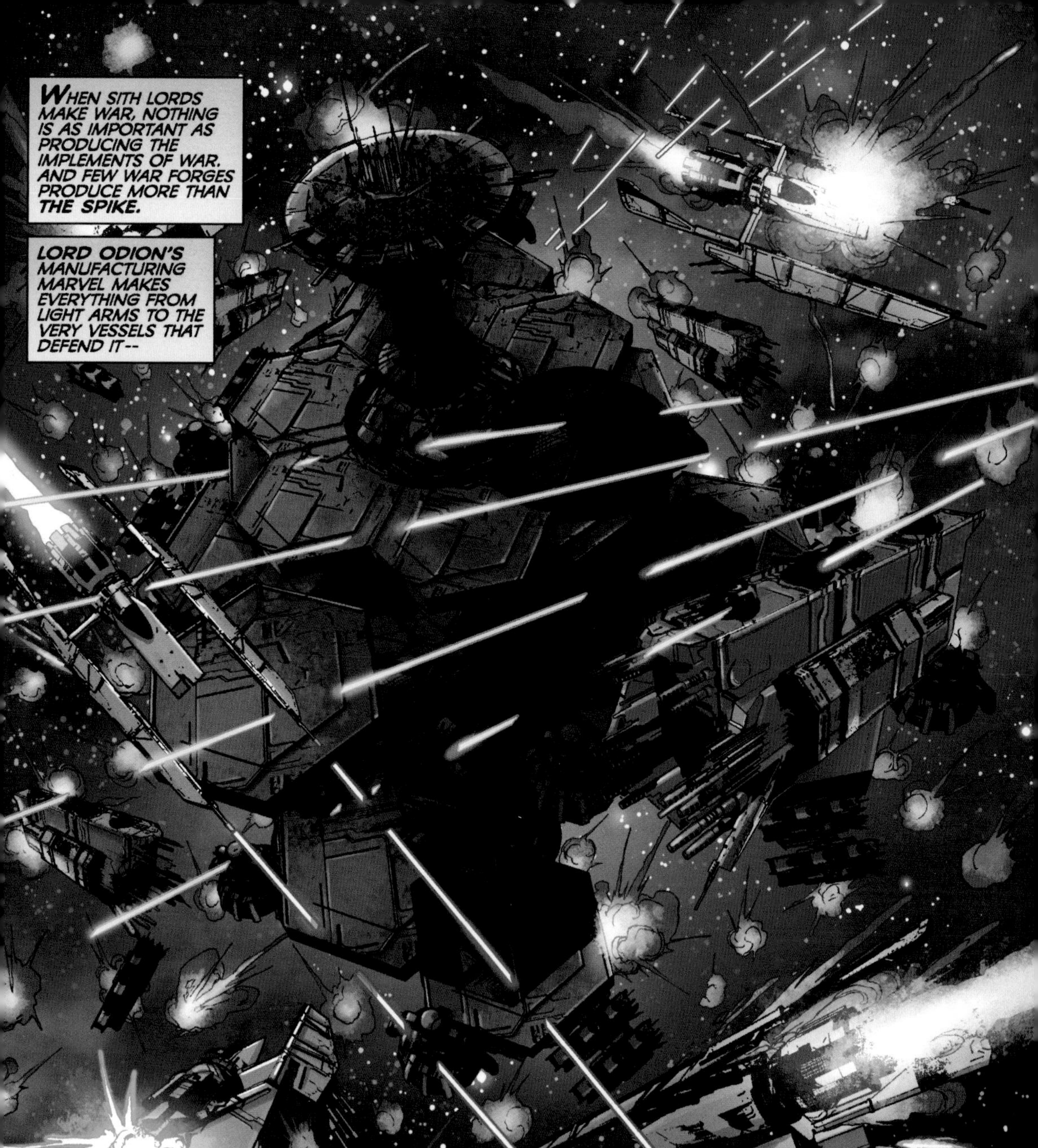
WHEN SITH LORDS MAKE WAR, NOTHING IS AS IMPORTANT AS PRODUCING THE IMPLEMENTS OF WAR. AND FEW WAR FORGES PRODUCE MORE THAN THE SPIKE.
LORD ODION'S MANUFACTURING MARVEL MAKES EVERYTHING FROM LIGHT ARMS TO THE VERY VESSELS THAT DEFEND IT--

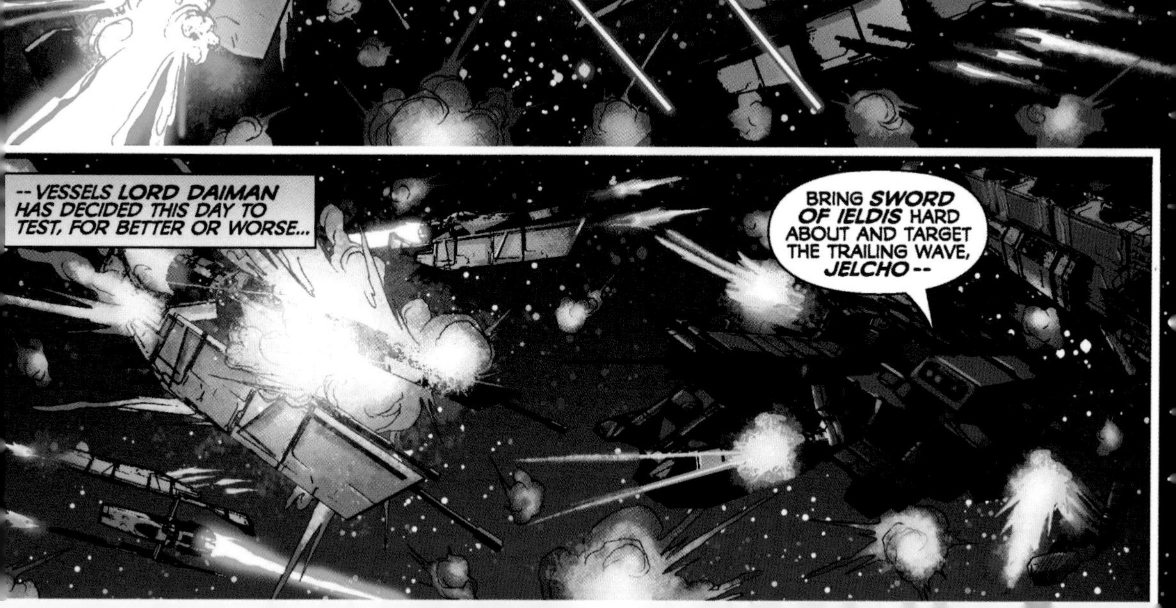
--VESSELS LORD DAIMAN HAS DECIDED THIS DAY TO TEST, FOR BETTER OR WORSE...
BRING SWORD OF IELDIS HARD ABOUT AND TARGET THE TRAILING WAVE, JELCHO--

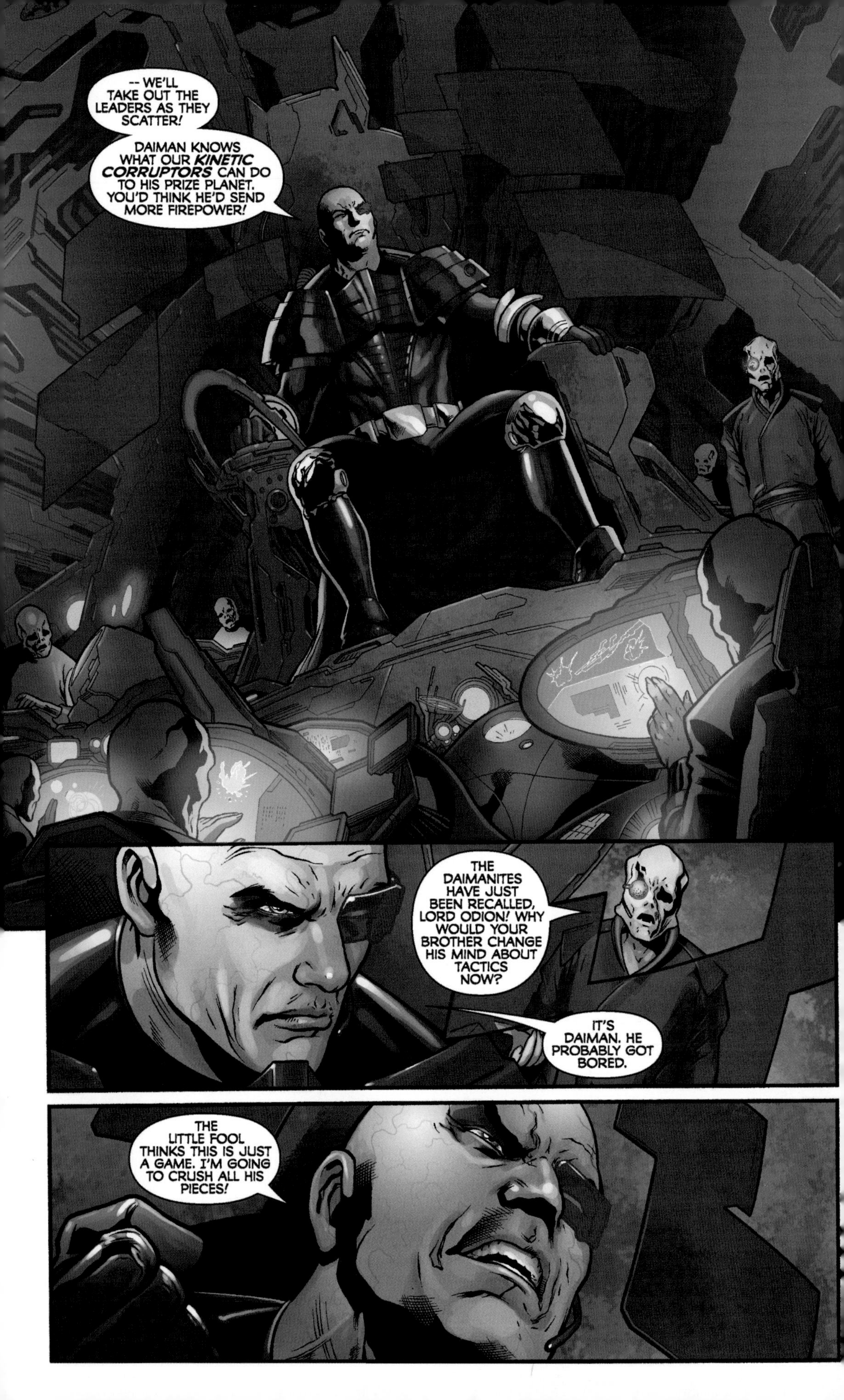
-- WE'LL TAKE OUT THE LEADERS AS THEY SCATTER!
DAIMAN KNOWS WHAT OUR KINETIC CORRUPTORS CAN DO TO HIS PRIZE PLANET. YOU'D THINK HE'D SEND MORE FIREPOWER!
THE DAIMANITES HAVE JUST BEEN RECALLED, LORD ODION! WHY WOULD YOUR BROTHER CHANGE HIS MIND ABOUT TACTICS NOW?
IT'S DAIMAN. HE PROBABLY GOT BORED.
THE LITTLE FOOL THINKS THIS IS JUST A GAME. I'M GOING TO CRUSH ALL HIS PIECES!

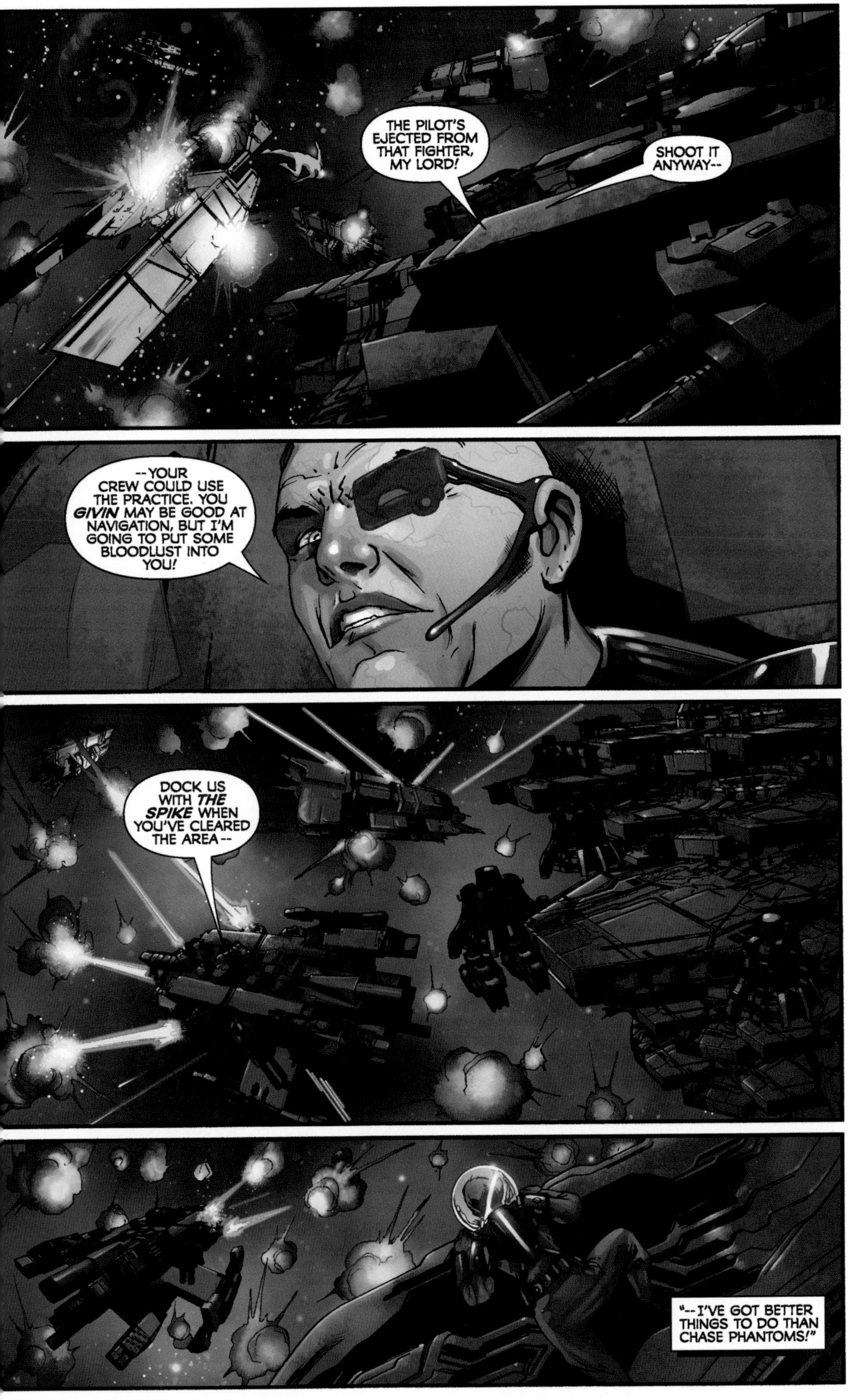
THE PILOT'S EJECTED FROM THAT FIGHTER, MY LORD!
SHOOT IT ANYWAY--
--YOUR CREW COULD USE THE PRACTICE. YOU *GIVIN* MAY BE GOOD AT NAVIGATION, BUT I'M GOING TO PUT SOME BLOODLUST INTO YOU!
DOCK US WITH *THE SPIKE* WHEN YOU'VE CLEARED THE AREA--
"--I'VE GOT BETTER THINGS TO DO THAN CHASE PHANTOMS!"

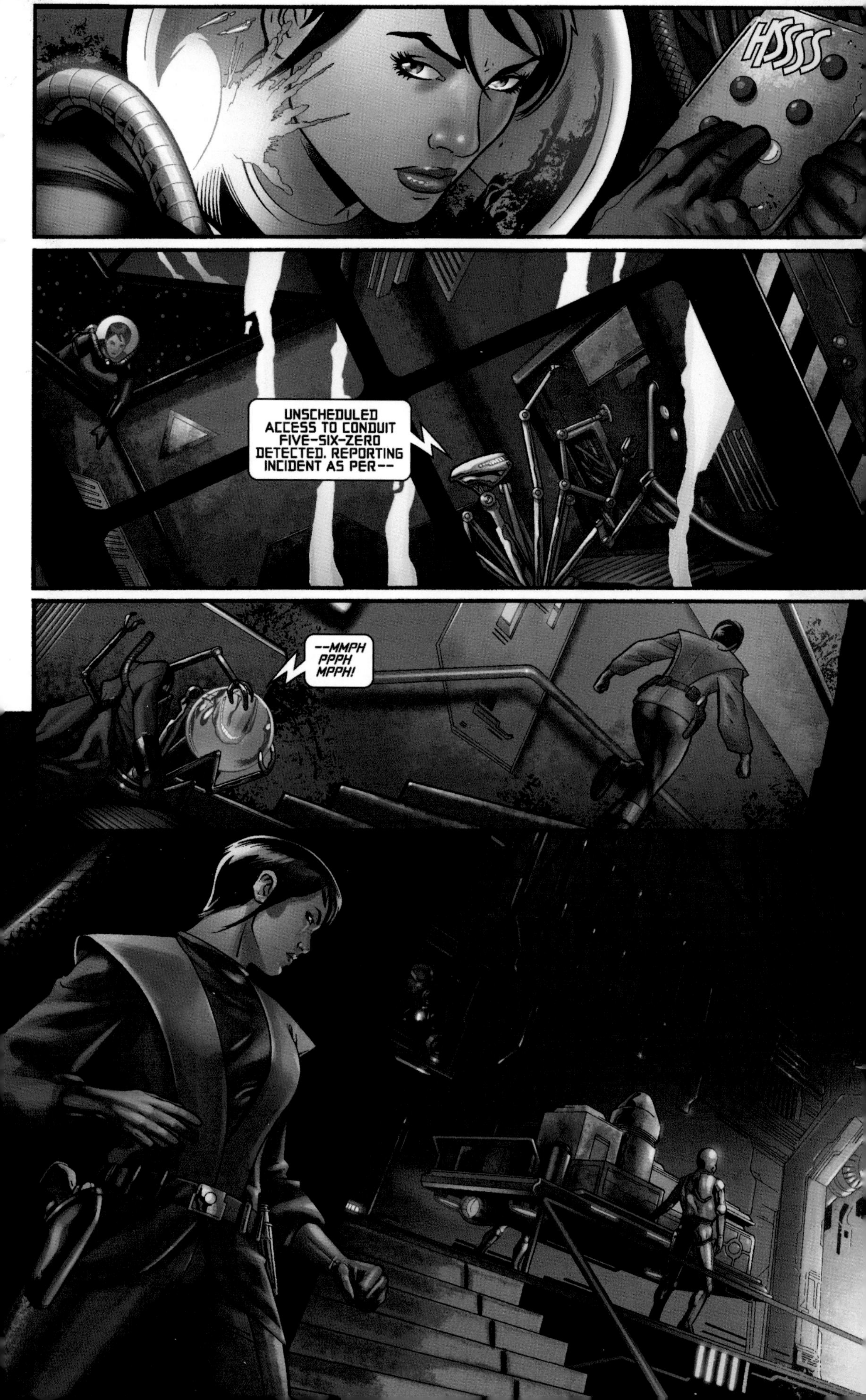
HSSSS
UNSCHEDULED ACCESS TO CONDUIT FIVE-SIX-ZERO DETECTED. REPORTING INCIDENT AS PER--
--MMPH PPPH MPPH!

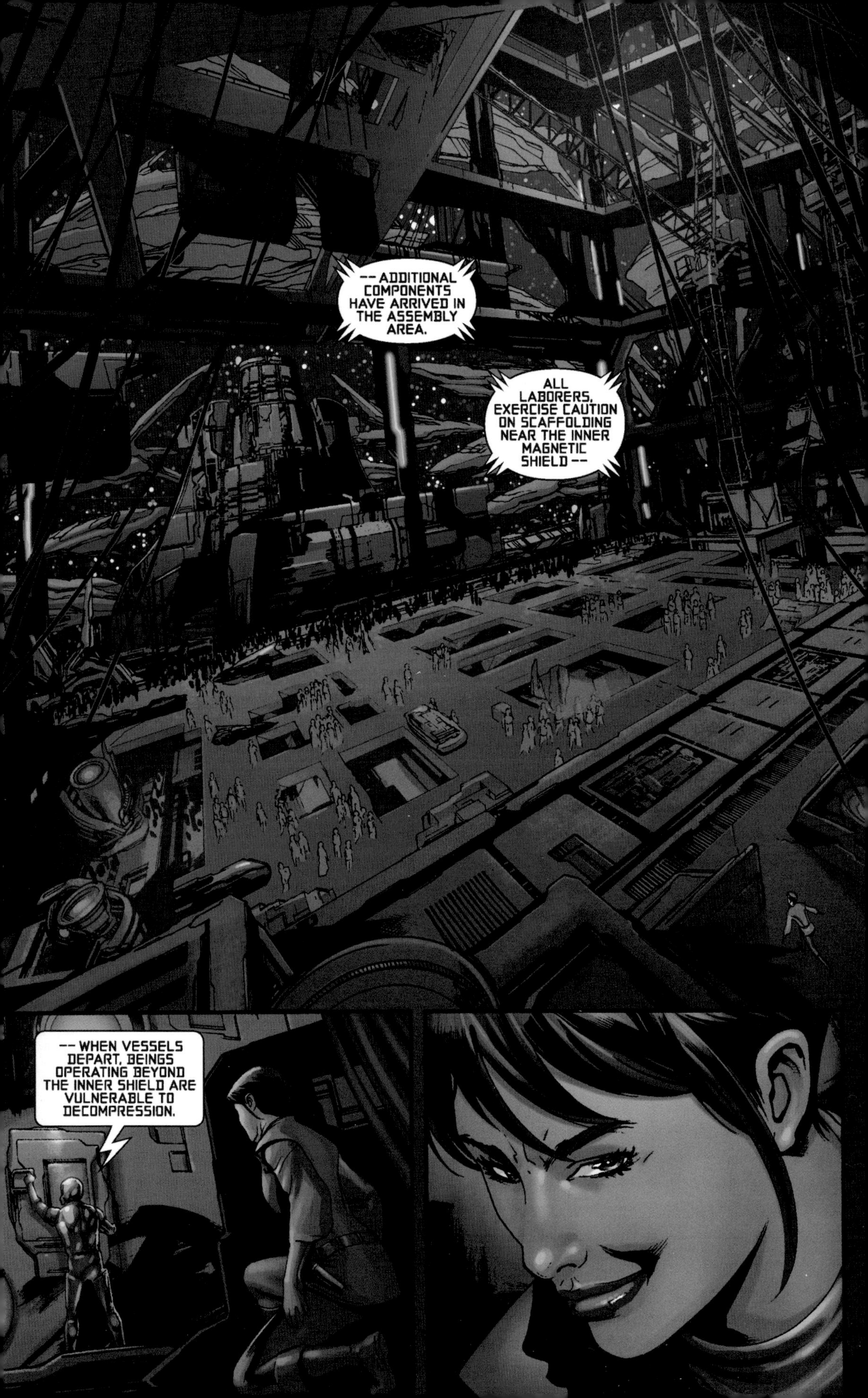

-- ADDITIONAL COMPONENTS HAVE ARRIVED IN THE ASSEMBLY AREA.
ALL LABORERS, EXERCISE CAUTION ON SCAFFOLDING NEAR THE INNER MAGNETIC SHIELD --
-- WHEN VESSELS DEPART, BEINGS OPERATING BEYOND THE INNER SHIELD ARE VULNERABLE TO DECOMPRESSION.

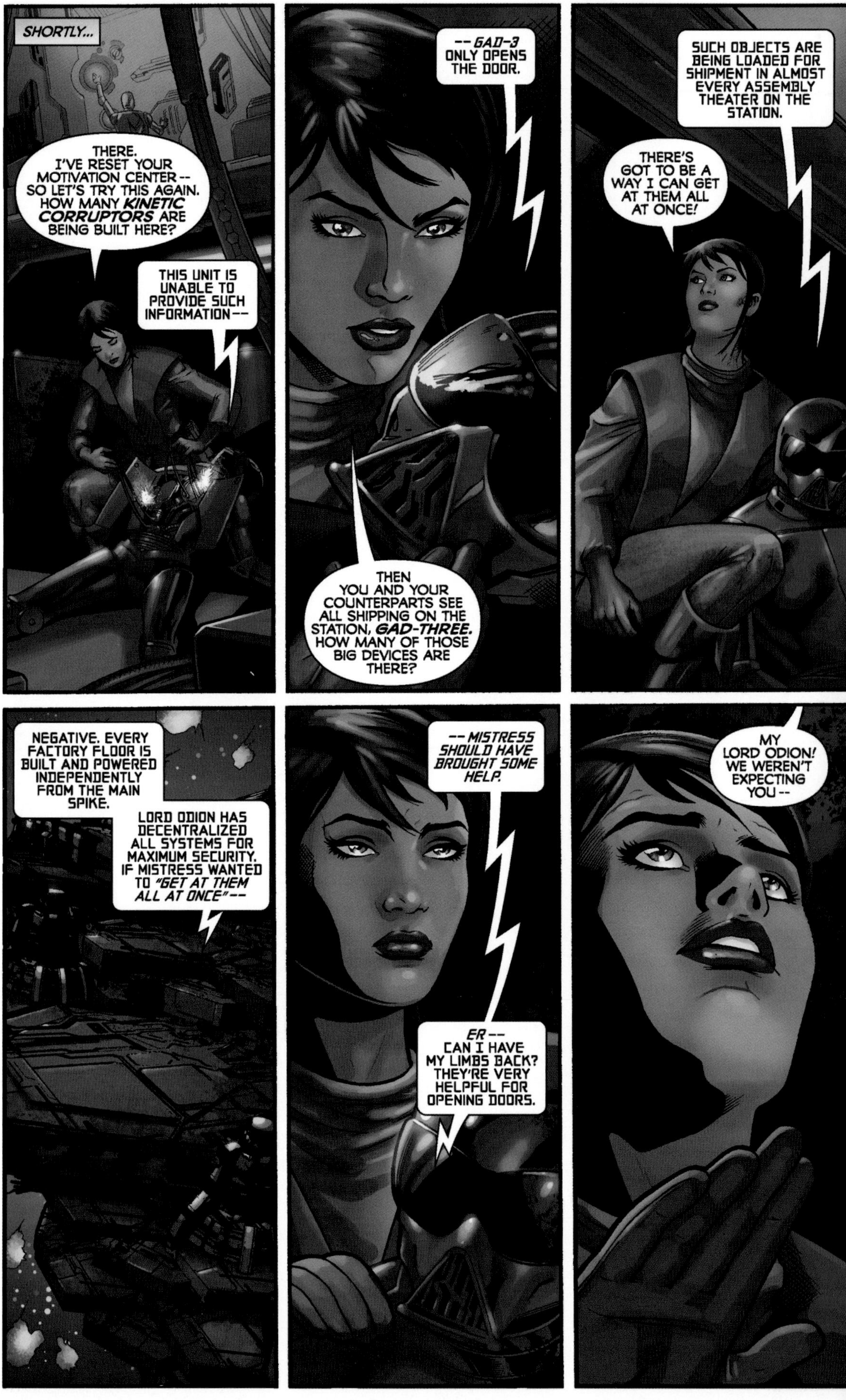
SHORTLY...
THERE. I'VE RESET YOUR MOTIVATION CENTER -- SO LET'S TRY THIS AGAIN. HOW MANY *KINETIC CORRUPTORS* ARE BEING BUILT HERE?
THIS UNIT IS UNABLE TO PROVIDE SUCH INFORMATION --
-- *GAD-3* ONLY OPENS THE DOOR.
THEN YOU AND YOUR COUNTERPARTS SEE ALL SHIPPING ON THE STATION, *GAD-THREE.* HOW MANY OF THOSE BIG DEVICES ARE THERE?
SUCH OBJECTS ARE BEING LOADED FOR SHIPMENT IN ALMOST EVERY ASSEMBLY THEATER ON THE STATION.
THERE'S GOT TO BE A WAY I CAN GET AT THEM ALL AT ONCE!
NEGATIVE. EVERY FACTORY FLOOR IS BUILT AND POWERED INDEPENDENTLY FROM THE MAIN SPIKE.
LORD ODION HAS DECENTRALIZED ALL SYSTEMS FOR MAXIMUM SECURITY. IF MISTRESS WANTED TO *"GET AT THEM ALL AT ONCE"* --
-- MISTRESS SHOULD HAVE BROUGHT SOME HELP.
ER -- CAN I HAVE MY LIMBS BACK? THEY'RE VERY HELPFUL FOR OPENING DOORS.
MY LORD ODION! WE WEREN'T EXPECTING YOU --

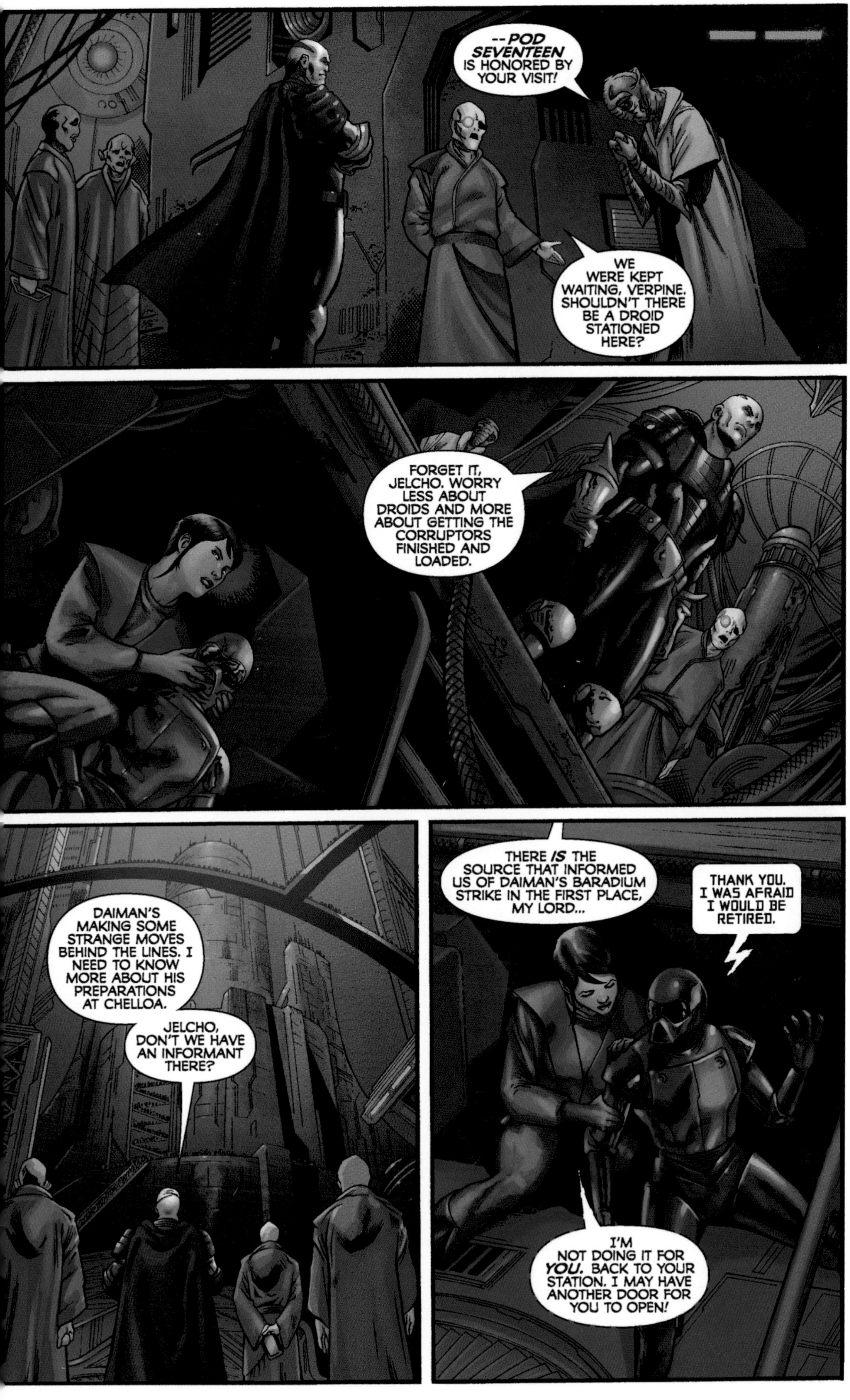
--POD SEVENTEEN IS HONORED BY YOUR VISIT!
WE WERE KEPT WAITING, VERPINE. SHOULDN'T THERE BE A DROID STATIONED HERE?
FORGET IT, JELCHO. WORRY LESS ABOUT DROIDS AND MORE ABOUT GETTING THE CORRUPTORS FINISHED AND LOADED.
DAIMAN'S MAKING SOME STRANGE MOVES BEHIND THE LINES. I NEED TO KNOW MORE ABOUT HIS PREPARATIONS AT CHELLOA.
JELCHO, DON'T WE HAVE AN INFORMANT THERE?
THERE *IS* THE SOURCE THAT INFORMED US OF DAIMAN'S BARADIUM STRIKE IN THE FIRST PLACE, MY LORD...
THANK YOU. I WAS AFRAID I WOULD BE RETIRED.
I'M NOT DOING IT FOR *YOU.* BACK TO YOUR STATION. I MAY HAVE ANOTHER DOOR FOR YOU TO OPEN!

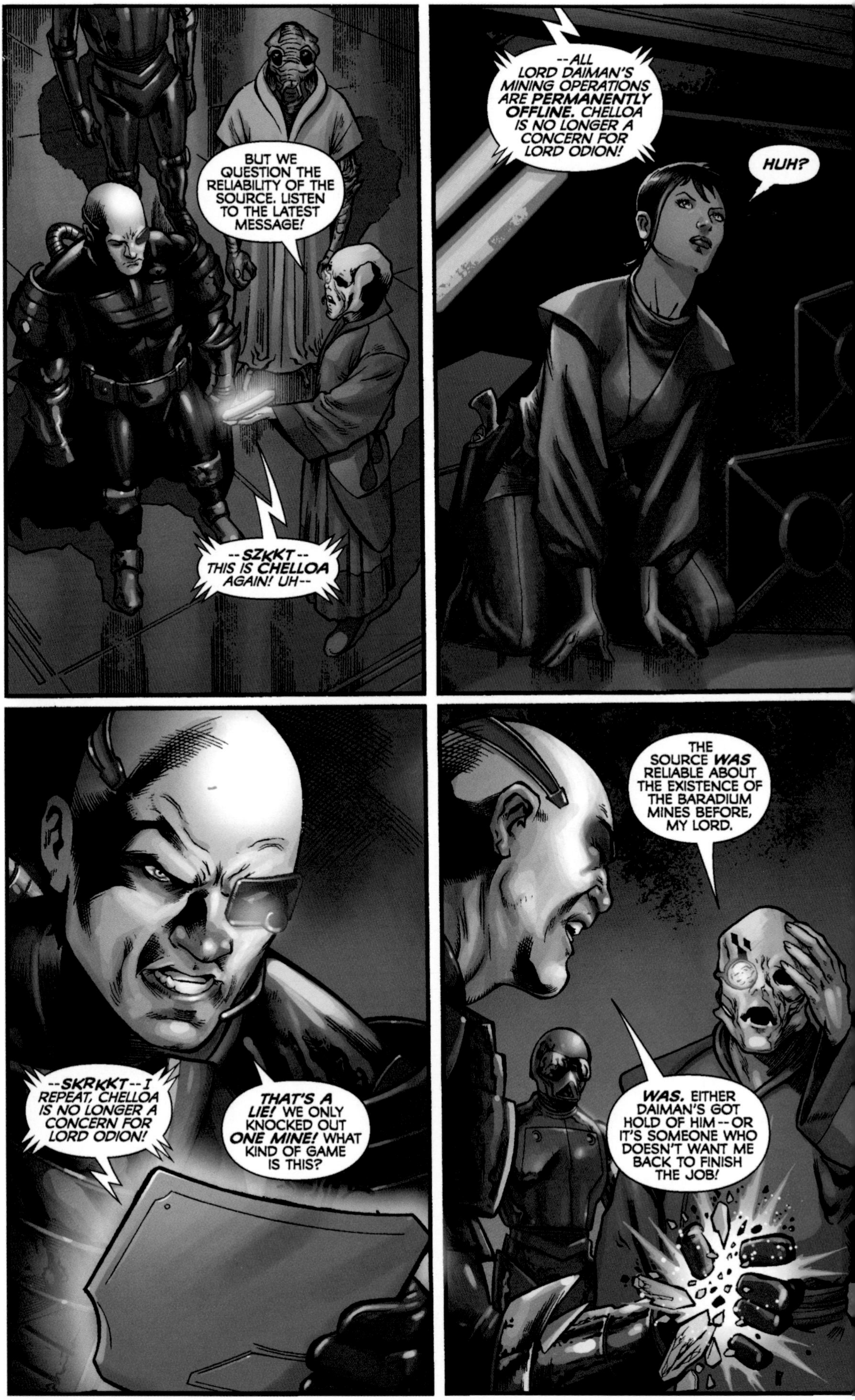
BUT WE QUESTION THE RELIABILITY OF THE SOURCE. LISTEN TO THE LATEST MESSAGE!
--SZKKT-- THIS IS CHELLOA AGAIN! UH--
--ALL LORD DAIMAN'S MINING OPERATIONS ARE PERMANENTLY OFFLINE. CHELLOA IS NO LONGER A CONCERN FOR LORD ODION!
HUH?
--SKRKKT--I REPEAT, CHELLOA IS NO LONGER A CONCERN FOR LORD ODION!
THAT'S A LIE! WE ONLY KNOCKED OUT ONE MINE! WHAT KIND OF GAME IS THIS?
THE SOURCE WAS RELIABLE ABOUT THE EXISTENCE OF THE BARADIUM MINES BEFORE, MY LORD.
WAS. EITHER DAIMAN'S GOT HOLD OF HIM--OR IT'S SOMEONE WHO DOESN'T WANT ME BACK TO FINISH THE JOB!

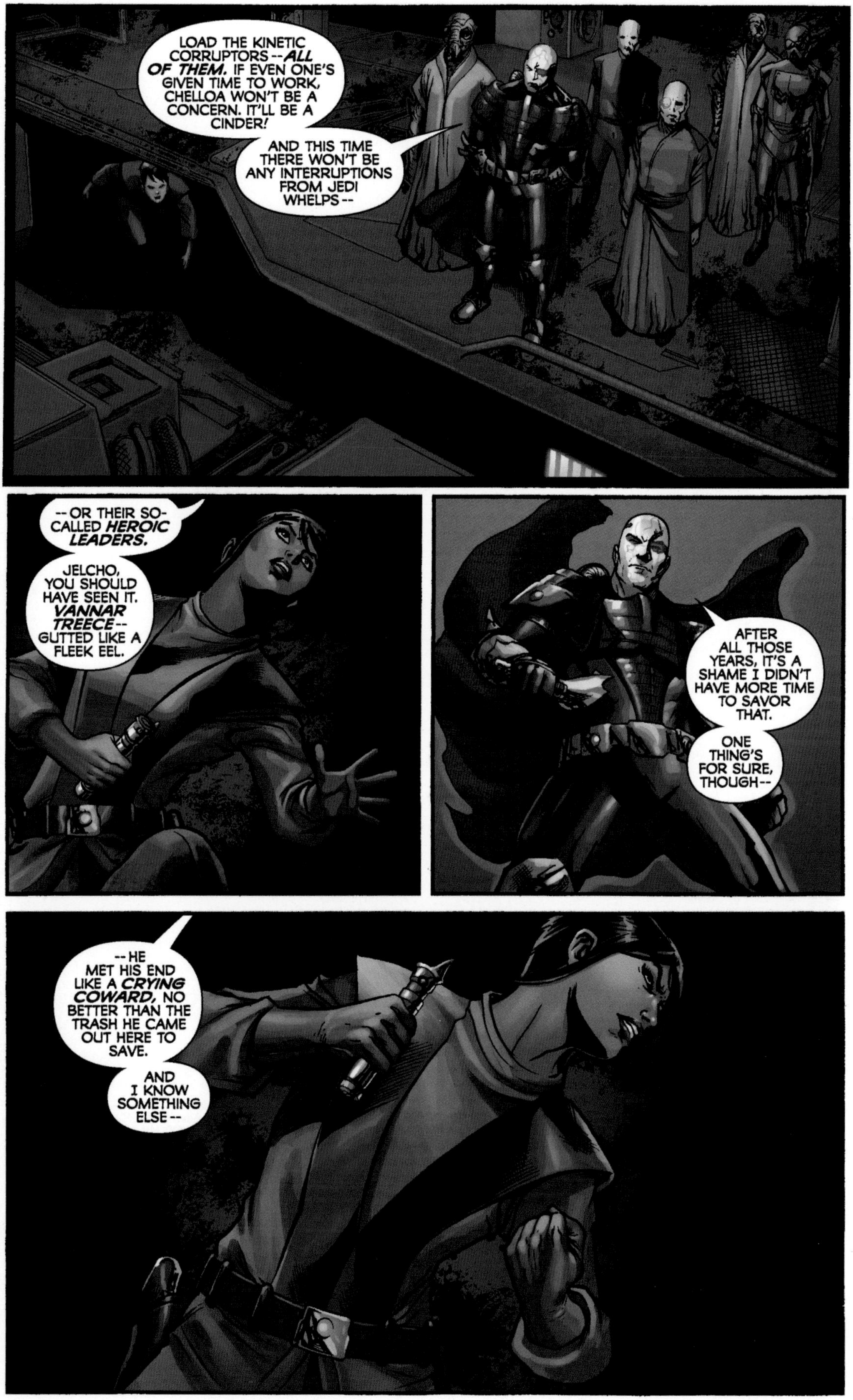
LOAD THE KINETIC CORRUPTORS--*ALL OF THEM.* IF EVEN ONE'S GIVEN TIME TO WORK, CHELLOA WON'T BE A CONCERN. IT'LL BE A CINDER!
AND THIS TIME THERE WON'T BE ANY INTERRUPTIONS FROM JEDI WHELPS--
--OR THEIR SO-CALLED *HEROIC LEADERS.*
JELCHO, YOU SHOULD HAVE SEEN IT. *VANNAR TREECE*--GUTTED LIKE A FLEEK EEL.
AFTER ALL THOSE YEARS, IT'S A SHAME I DIDN'T HAVE MORE TIME TO SAVOR THAT.
ONE THING'S FOR SURE, THOUGH--
--HE MET HIS END LIKE A *CRYING COWARD,* NO BETTER THAN THE TRASH HE CAME OUT HERE TO SAVE.
AND I KNOW SOMETHING ELSE--

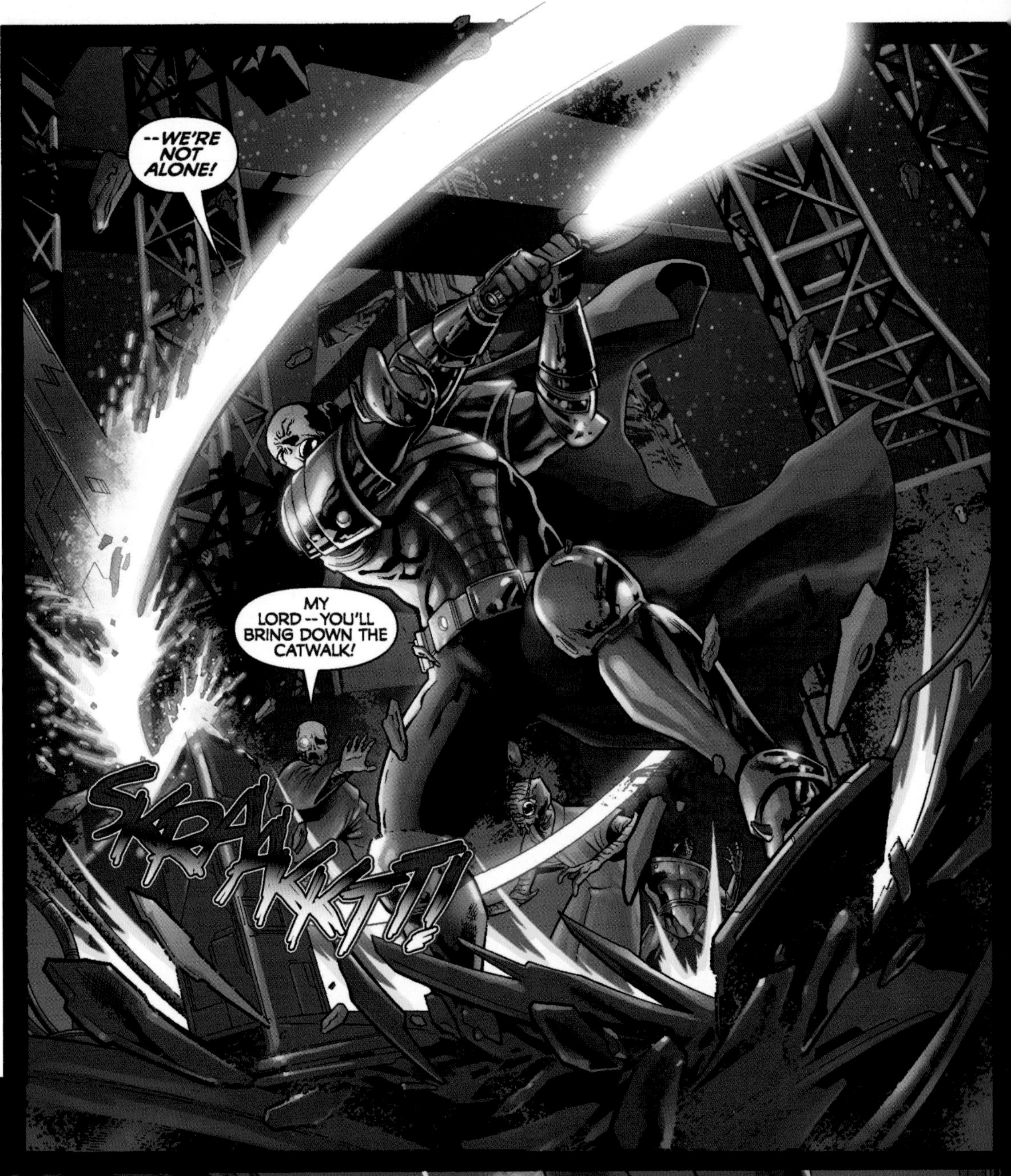
--WE'RE NOT ALONE!
MY LORD--YOU'LL BRING DOWN THE CATWALK!
SKRAAKKKTT!

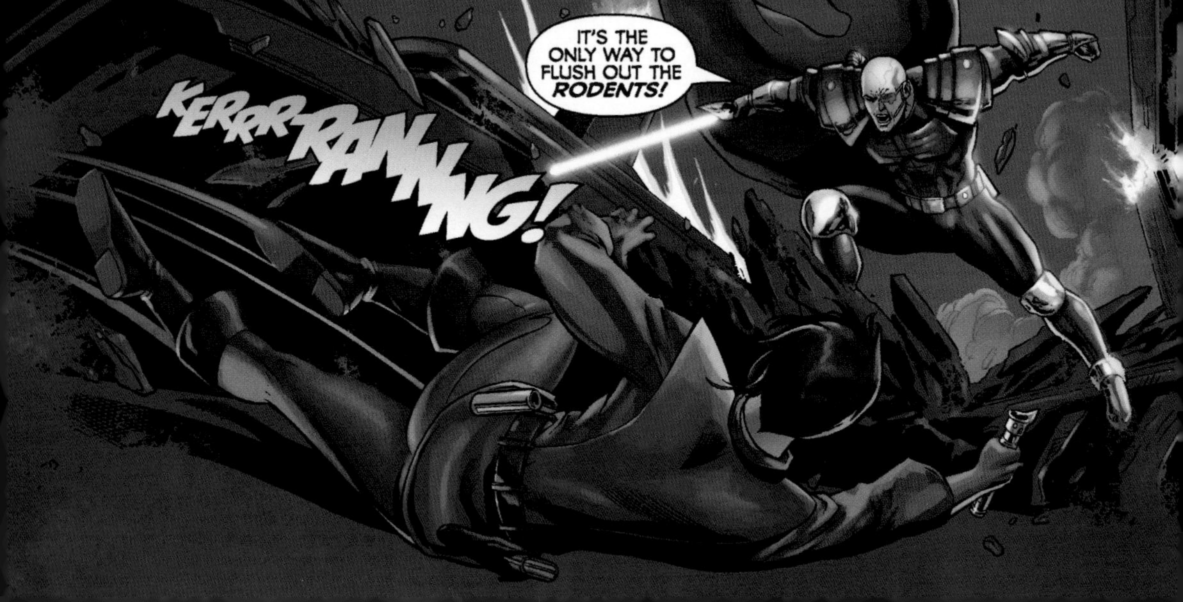
IT'S THE ONLY WAY TO FLUSH OUT THE *RODENTS!*
KERRR-RANNNG!

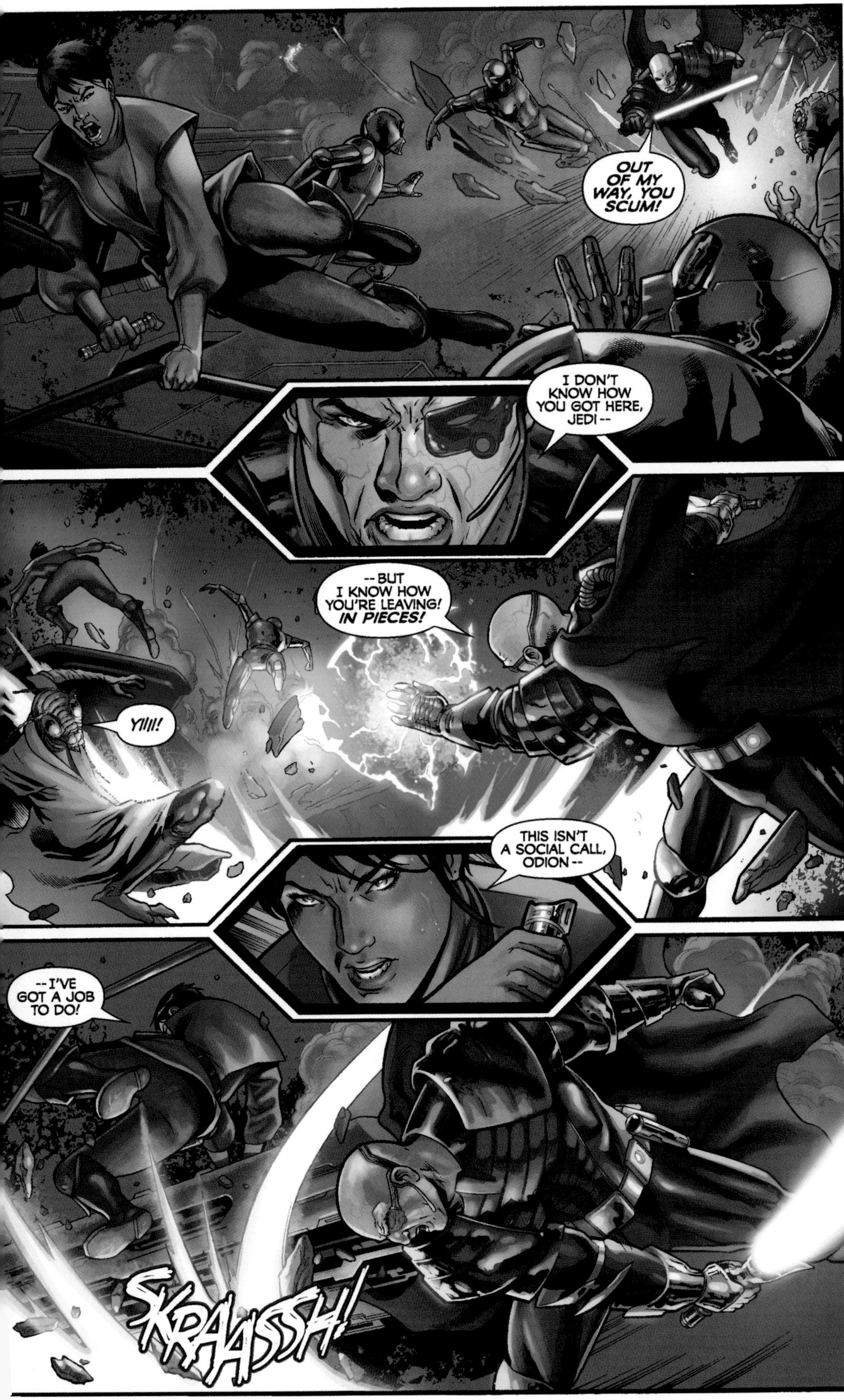
OUT OF MY WAY, YOU SCUM!
I DON'T KNOW HOW YOU GOT HERE, JEDI --
-- BUT I KNOW HOW YOU'RE LEAVING! IN PIECES!
YIIII!
THIS ISN'T A SOCIAL CALL, ODION --
-- I'VE GOT A JOB TO DO!
SKRAASSH!

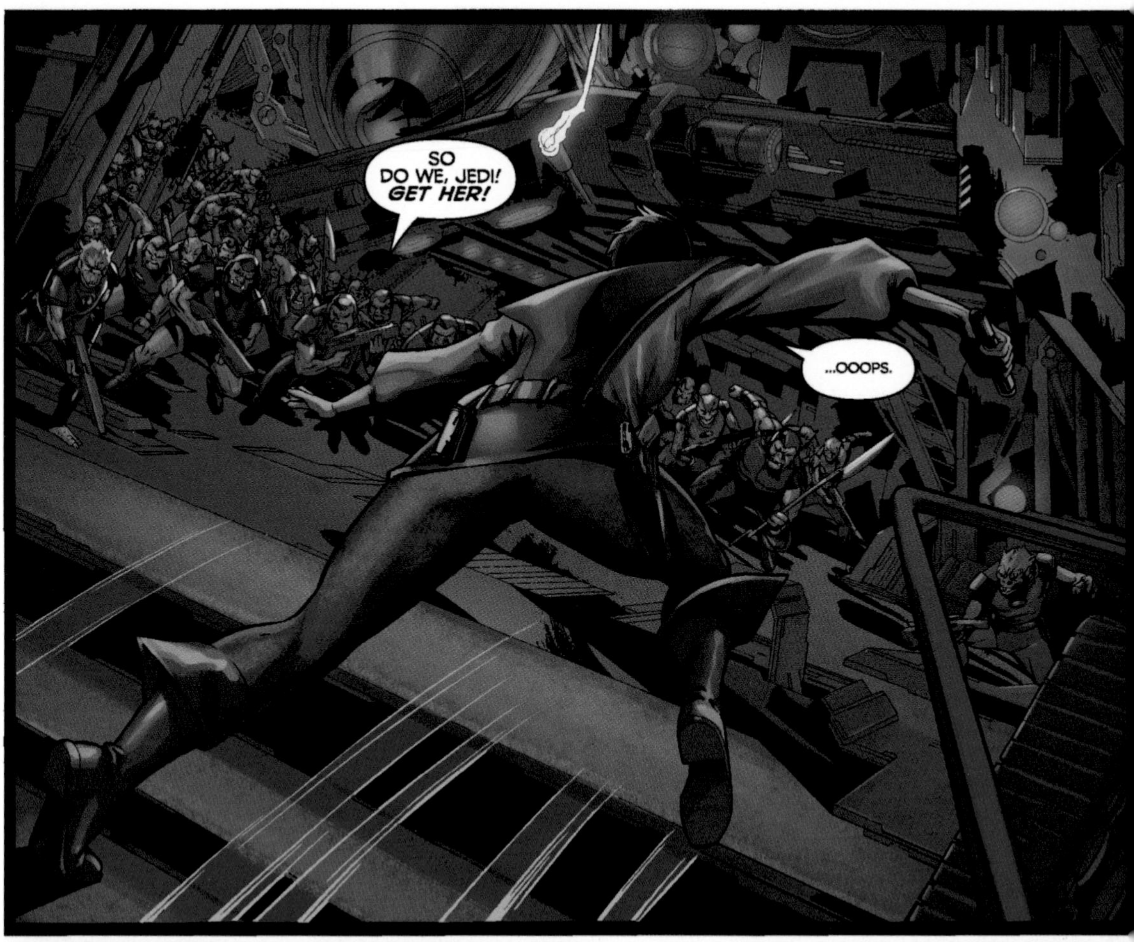
SO
DO WE, JEDI!
GET HER!
...OOOPS.

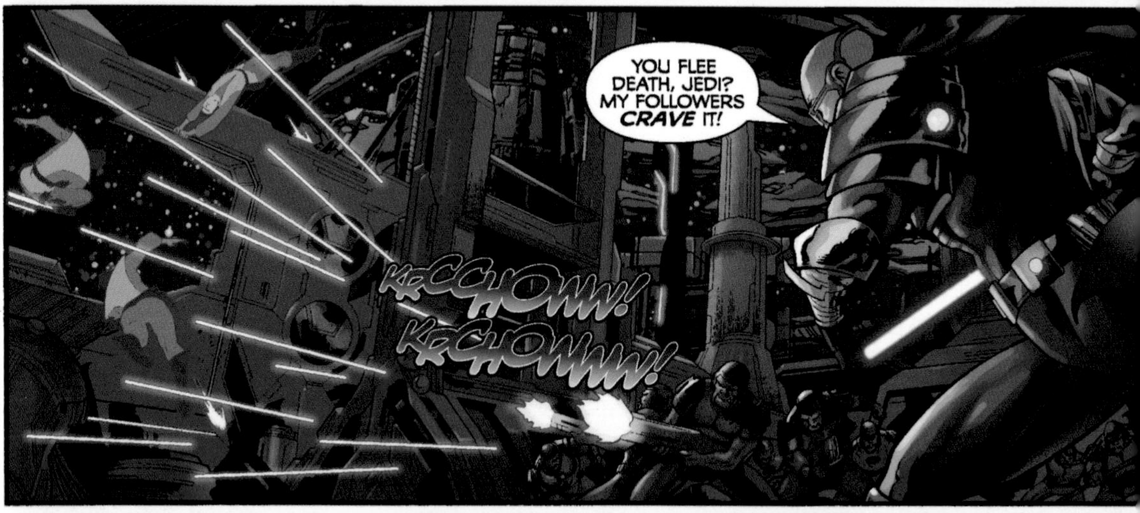
YOU FLEE DEATH, JEDI? MY FOLLOWERS CRAVE IT!
KRCCHOWW!
KRCHOWWW!

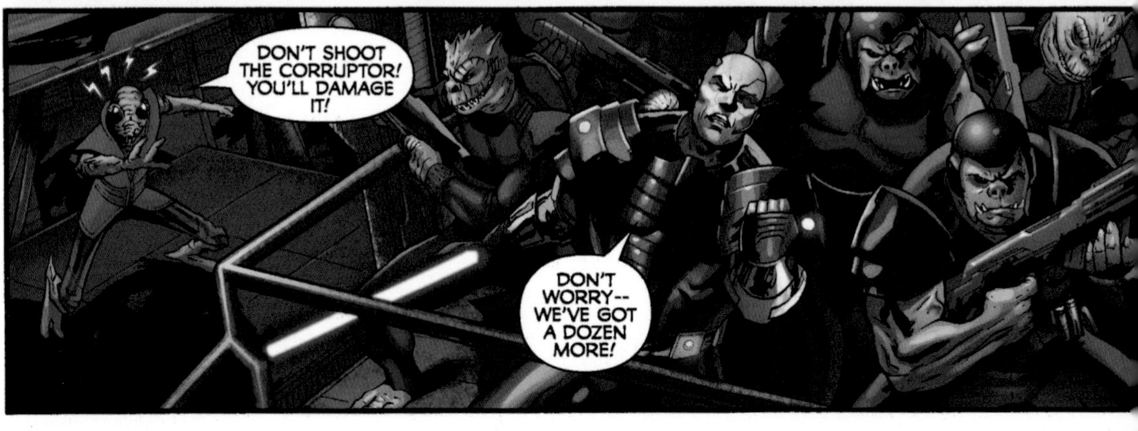
DON'T SHOOT THE CORRUPTOR! YOU'LL DAMAGE IT!
DON'T WORRY-- WE'VE GOT A DOZEN MORE!

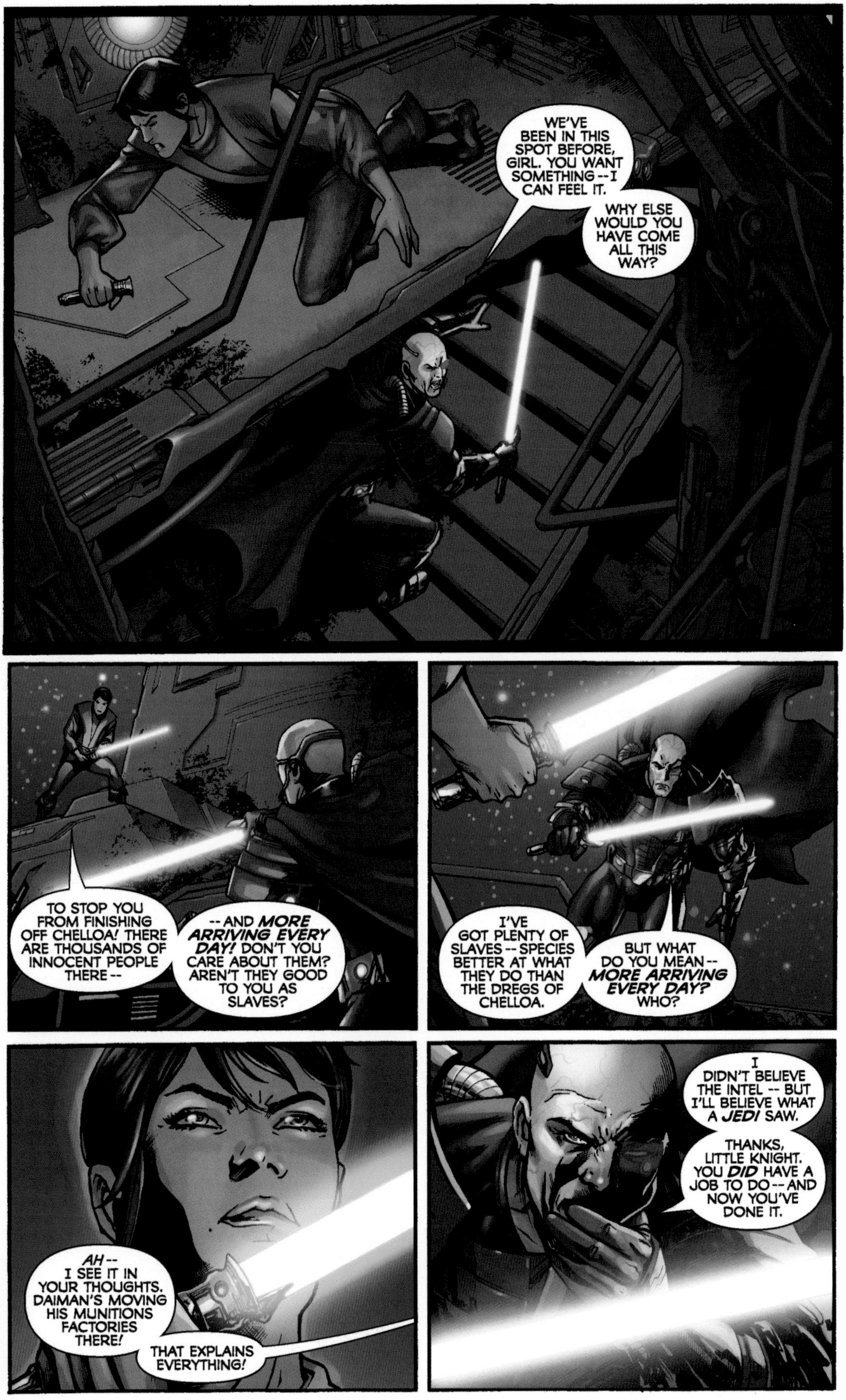
WE'VE BEEN IN THIS SPOT BEFORE, GIRL. YOU WANT SOMETHING -- I CAN FEEL IT.
WHY ELSE WOULD YOU HAVE COME ALL THIS WAY?
TO STOP YOU FROM FINISHING OFF CHELLOA! THERE ARE THOUSANDS OF INNOCENT PEOPLE THERE --
-- AND MORE ARRIVING EVERY DAY! DON'T YOU CARE ABOUT THEM? AREN'T THEY GOOD TO YOU AS SLAVES?
I'VE GOT PLENTY OF SLAVES -- SPECIES BETTER AT WHAT THEY DO THAN THE DREGS OF CHELLOA.
BUT WHAT DO YOU MEAN -- MORE ARRIVING EVERY DAY? WHO?
AH -- I SEE IT IN YOUR THOUGHTS. DAIMAN'S MOVING HIS MUNITIONS FACTORIES THERE!
THAT EXPLAINS EVERYTHING!
I DIDN'T BELIEVE THE INTEL -- BUT I'LL BELIEVE WHAT A JEDI SAW.
THANKS, LITTLE KNIGHT. YOU DID HAVE A JOB TO DO -- AND NOW YOU'VE DONE IT.

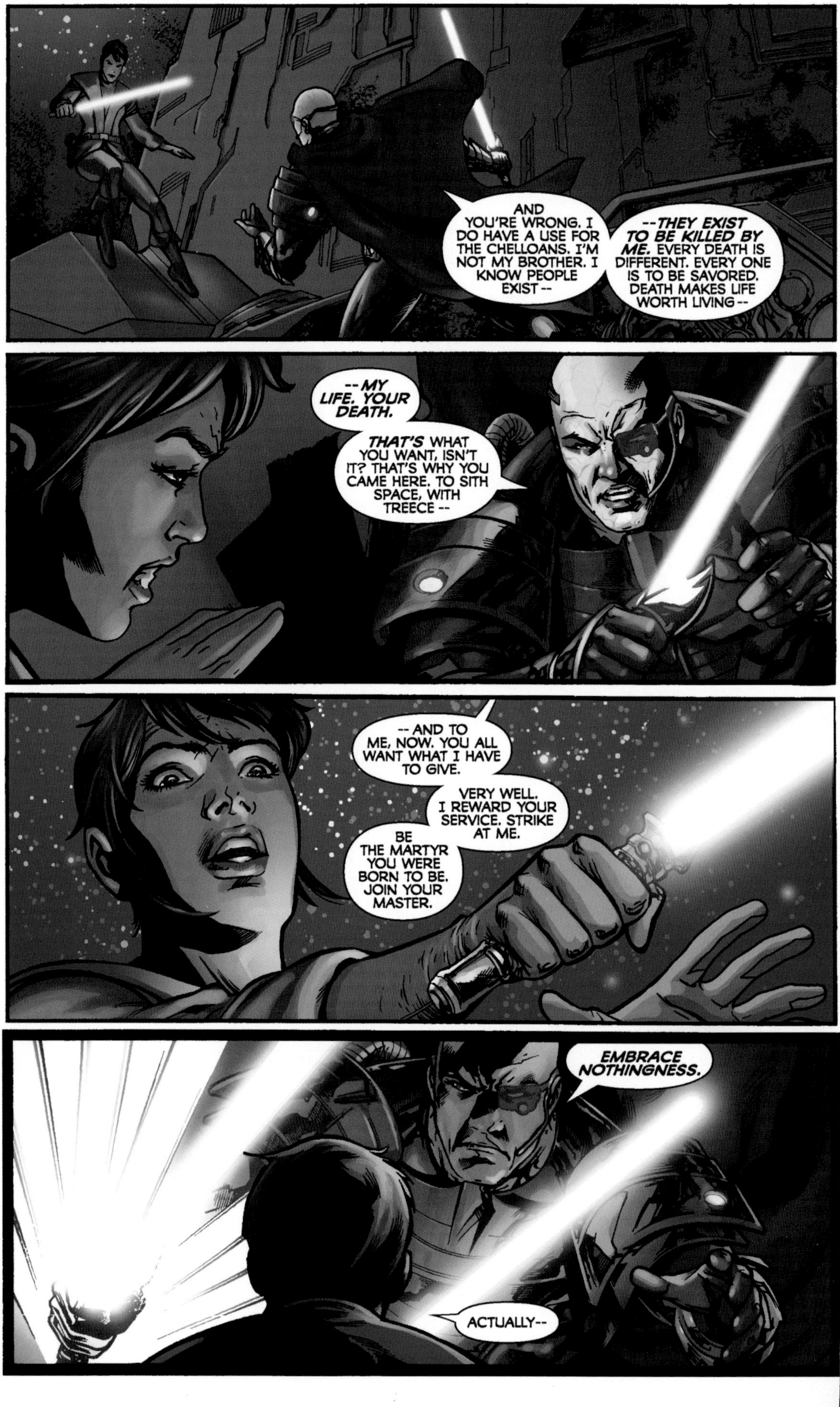
AND YOU'RE WRONG. I DO HAVE A USE FOR THE CHELLOANS. I'M NOT MY BROTHER. I KNOW PEOPLE EXIST --
--*THEY EXIST TO BE KILLED BY ME.* EVERY DEATH IS DIFFERENT. EVERY ONE IS TO BE SAVORED. DEATH MAKES LIFE WORTH LIVING --
-- *MY LIFE. YOUR DEATH.*
THAT'S WHAT YOU WANT, ISN'T IT? THAT'S WHY YOU CAME HERE. TO SITH SPACE, WITH TREECE --
-- AND TO ME, NOW. YOU ALL WANT WHAT I HAVE TO GIVE.
VERY WELL. I REWARD YOUR SERVICE. STRIKE AT ME.
BE THE MARTYR YOU WERE BORN TO BE. JOIN YOUR MASTER.
EMBRACE NOTHINGNESS.
ACTUALLY--

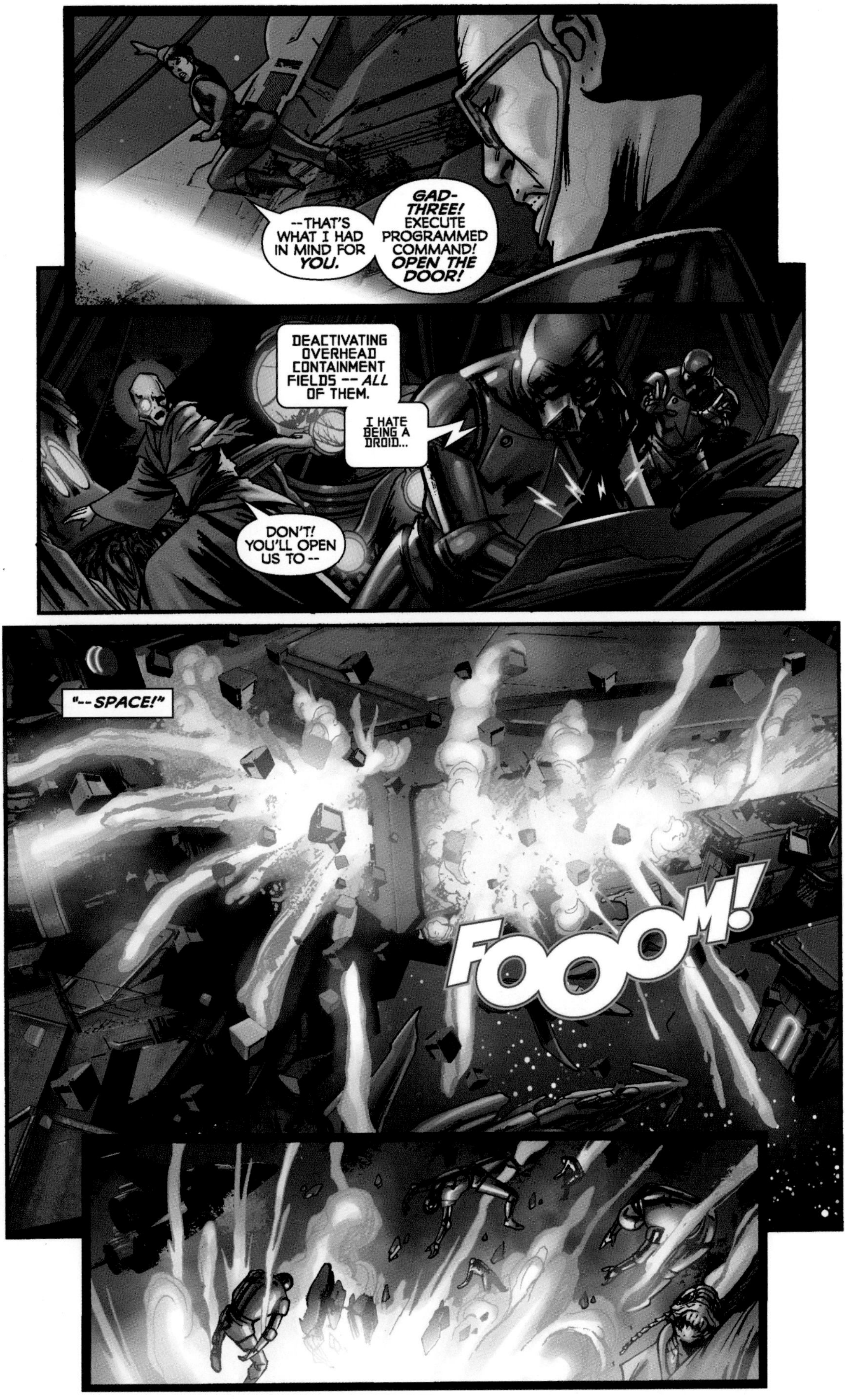
--THAT'S WHAT I HAD IN MIND FOR *YOU.*
GAD-THREE! EXECUTE PROGRAMMED COMMAND! *OPEN THE DOOR!*
DEACTIVATING OVERHEAD CONTAINMENT FIELDS -- *ALL* OF THEM.
I HATE BEING A DROID...
DON'T! YOU'LL OPEN US TO --
"--*SPACE!*"
FOOOM!

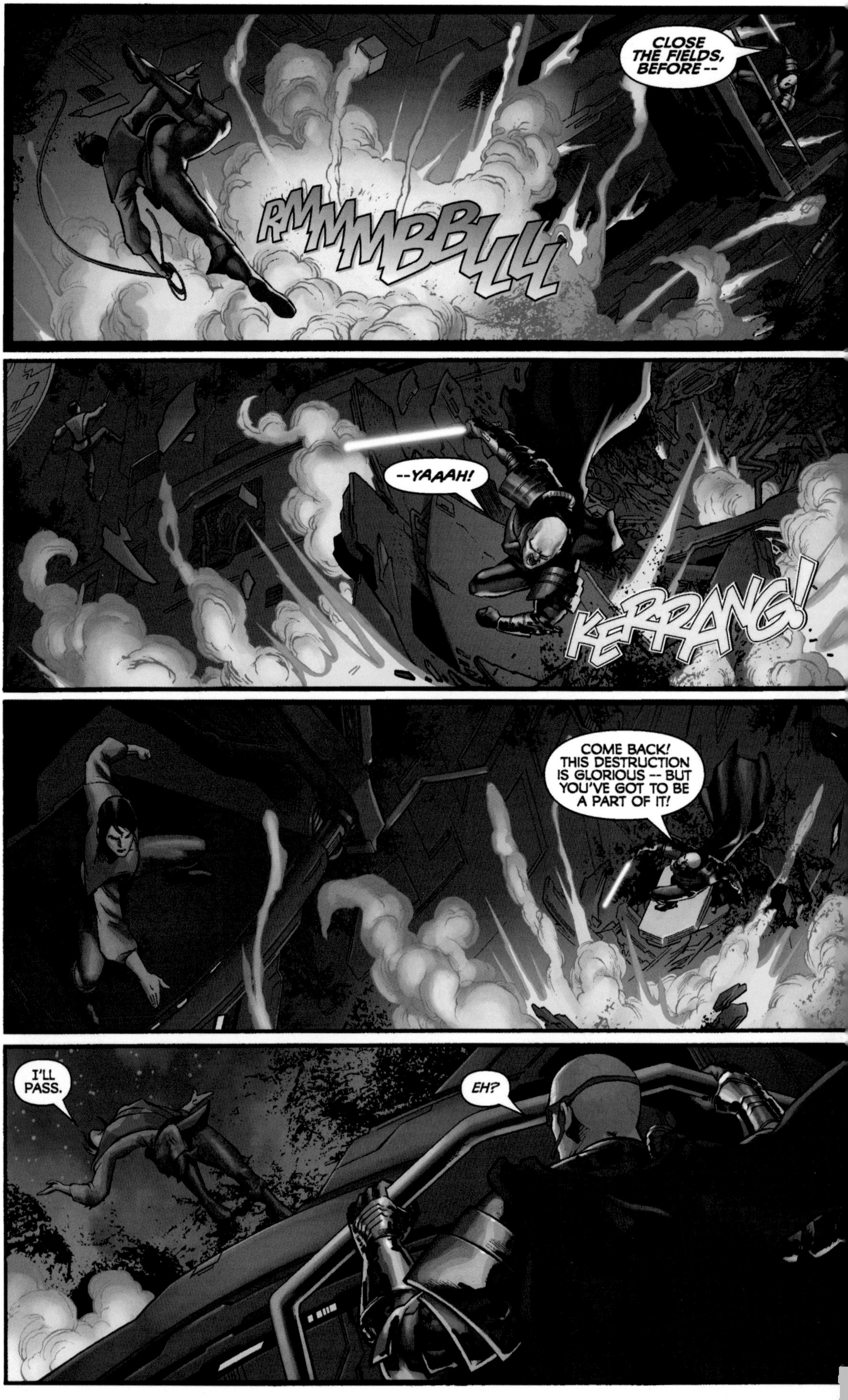
CLOSE THE FIELDS, BEFORE --
RMMMBBLLLL
--YAAAH!
KERRANG!
COME BACK! THIS DESTRUCTION IS GLORIOUS -- BUT YOU'VE GOT TO BE A PART OF IT!
I'LL PASS.
EH?

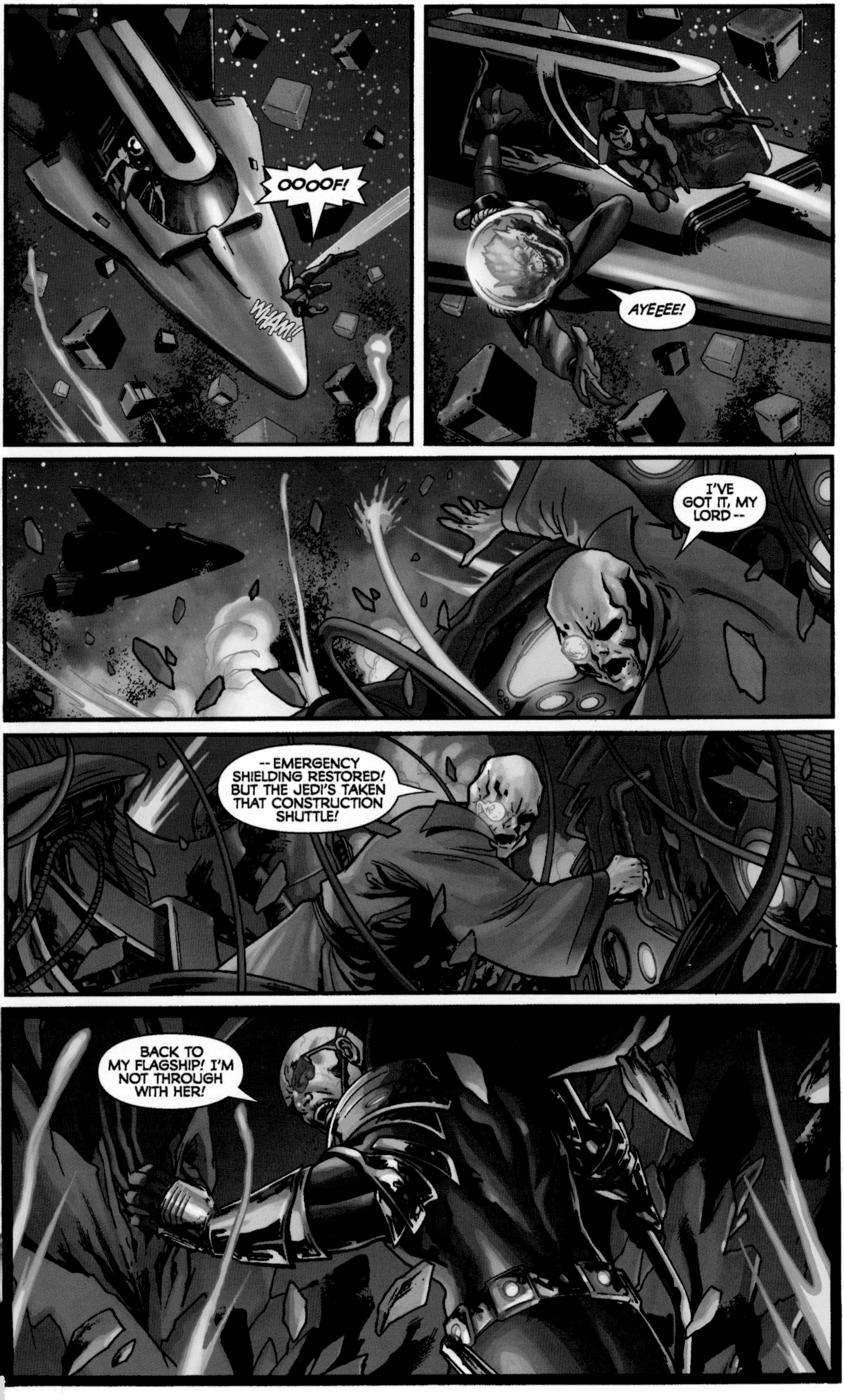
OOOOF!
WHAM!
AYEEEE!
I'VE GOT IT, MY LORD --
-- EMERGENCY SHIELDING RESTORED! BUT THE JEDI'S TAKEN THAT CONSTRUCTION SHUTTLE!
BACK TO MY FLAGSHIP! I'M NOT THROUGH WITH HER!

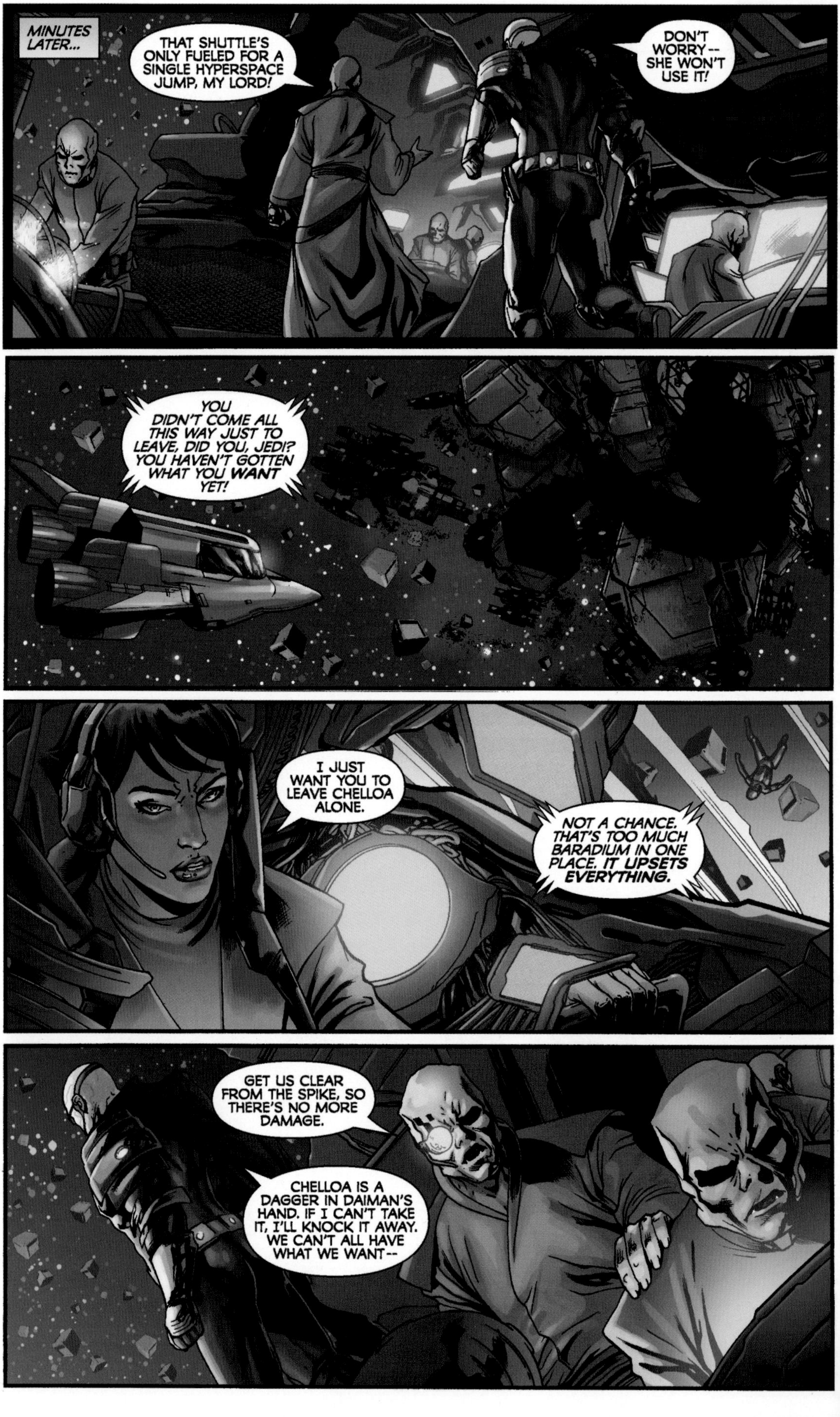
MINUTES LATER...
THAT SHUTTLE'S ONLY FUELED FOR A SINGLE HYPERSPACE JUMP, MY LORD!
DON'T WORRY-- SHE WON'T USE IT!
YOU DIDN'T COME ALL THIS WAY JUST TO LEAVE, DID YOU, JEDI? YOU HAVEN'T GOTTEN WHAT YOU WANT YET!
I JUST WANT YOU TO LEAVE CHELLOA ALONE.
NOT A CHANCE. THAT'S TOO MUCH BARADIUM IN ONE PLACE. IT UPSETS EVERYTHING.
GET US CLEAR FROM THE SPIKE, SO THERE'S NO MORE DAMAGE.
CHELLOA IS A DAGGER IN DAIMAN'S HAND. IF I CAN'T TAKE IT, I'LL KNOCK IT AWAY. WE CAN'T ALL HAVE WHAT WE WANT--

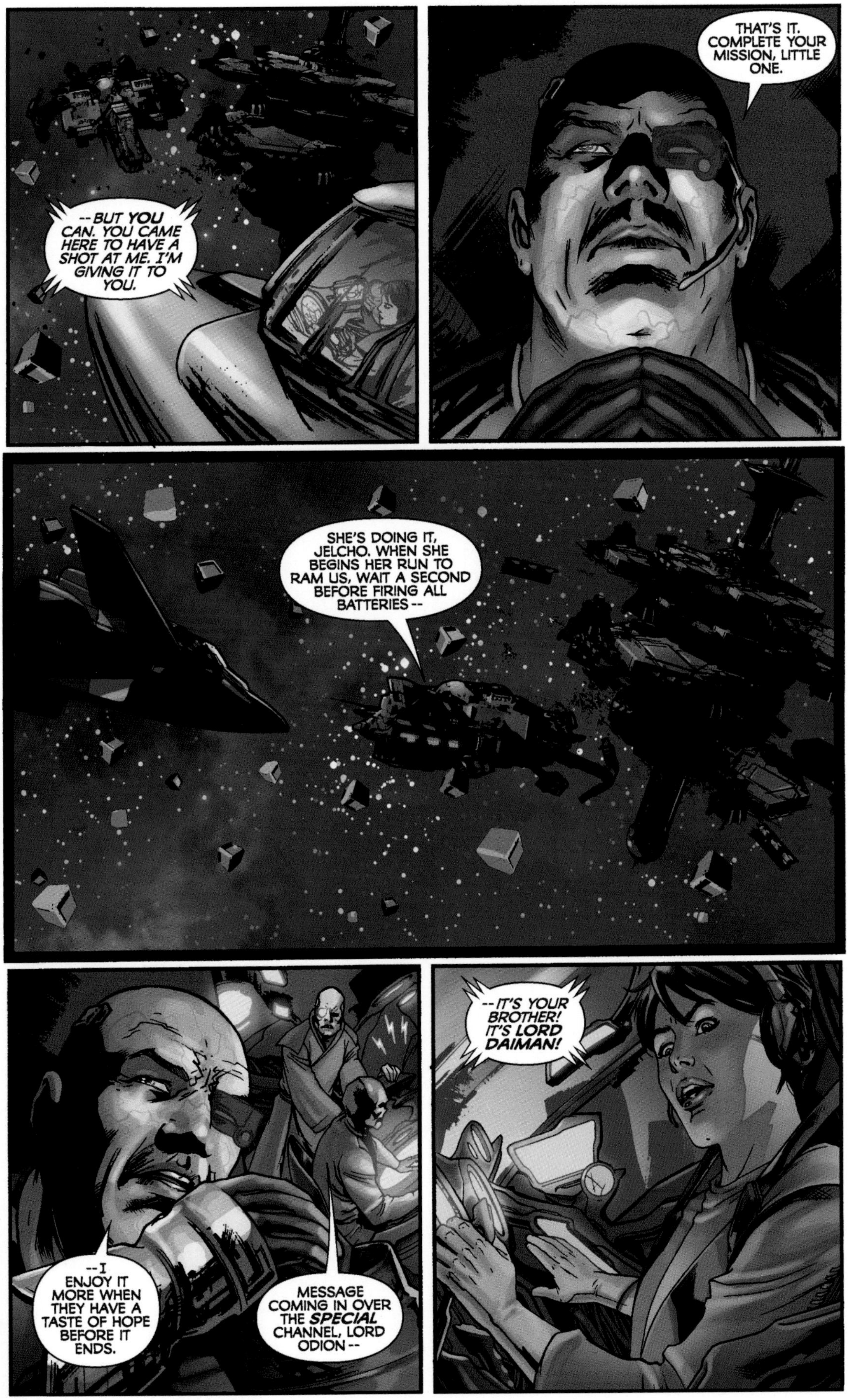
--BUT YOU CAN. YOU CAME HERE TO HAVE A SHOT AT ME. I'M GIVING IT TO YOU.
THAT'S IT. COMPLETE YOUR MISSION, LITTLE ONE.
SHE'S DOING IT, JELCHO. WHEN SHE BEGINS HER RUN TO RAM US, WAIT A SECOND BEFORE FIRING ALL BATTERIES--
--I ENJOY IT MORE WHEN THEY HAVE A TASTE OF HOPE BEFORE IT ENDS.
MESSAGE COMING IN OVER THE SPECIAL CHANNEL, LORD ODION--
--IT'S YOUR BROTHER! IT'S LORD DAIMAN!

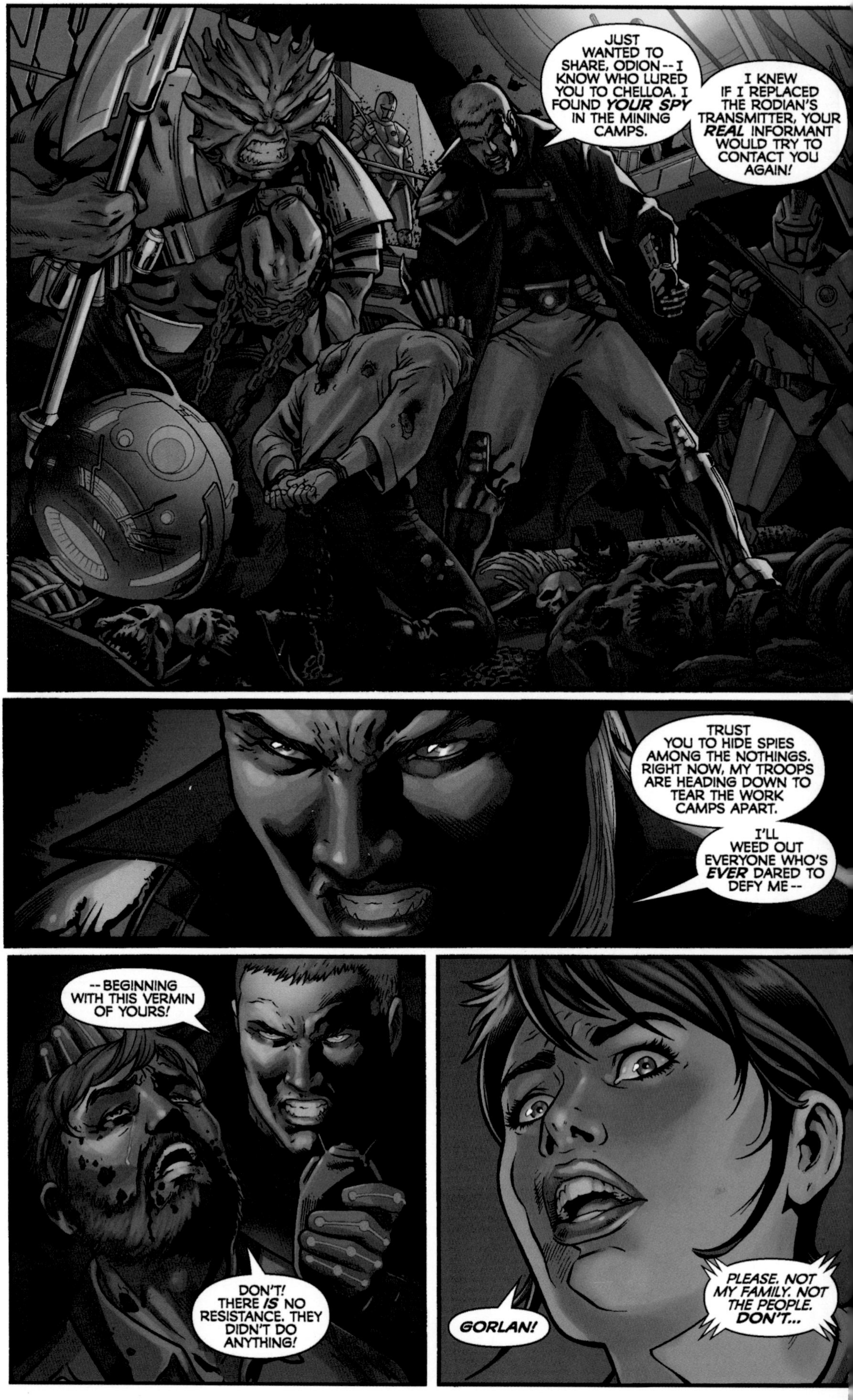
JUST WANTED TO SHARE, ODION -- I KNOW WHO LURED YOU TO CHELLOA. I FOUND YOUR SPY IN THE MINING CAMPS.
I KNEW IF I REPLACED THE RODIAN'S TRANSMITTER, YOUR REAL INFORMANT WOULD TRY TO CONTACT YOU AGAIN!
TRUST YOU TO HIDE SPIES AMONG THE NOTHINGS. RIGHT NOW, MY TROOPS ARE HEADING DOWN TO TEAR THE WORK CAMPS APART.
I'LL WEED OUT EVERYONE WHO'S EVER DARED TO DEFY ME --
-- BEGINNING WITH THIS VERMIN OF YOURS!
DON'T! THERE IS NO RESISTANCE. THEY DIDN'T DO ANYTHING!
GORLAN!
PLEASE. NOT MY FAMILY. NOT THE PEOPLE. DON'T...

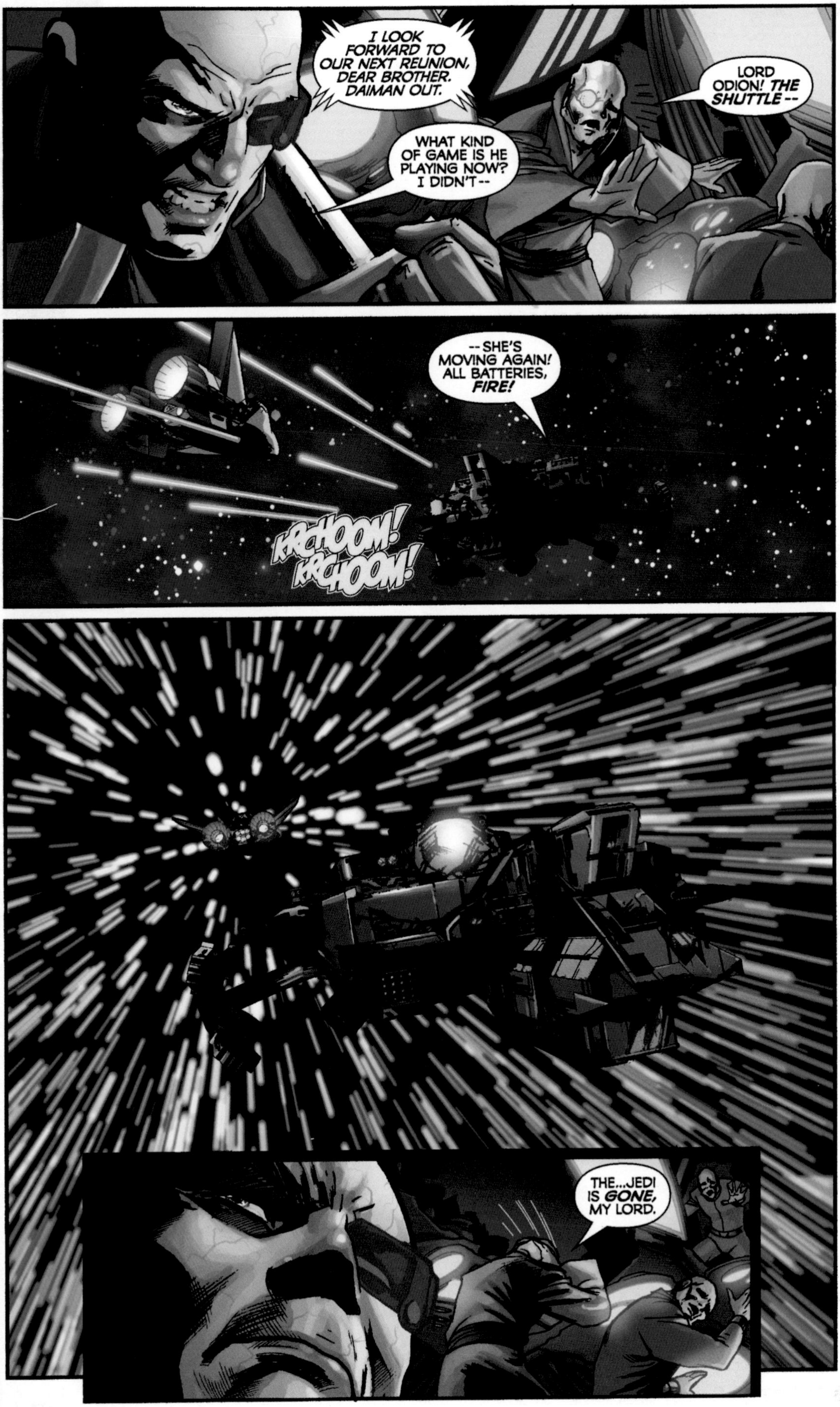
I LOOK FORWARD TO OUR NEXT REUNION, DEAR BROTHER. DAIMAN OUT.
WHAT KIND OF GAME IS HE PLAYING NOW? I DIDN'T--
LORD ODION! THE SHUTTLE--
--SHE'S MOVING AGAIN! ALL BATTERIES, FIRE!
KRCHOOM! KRCHOOM!
THE...JEDI IS GONE, MY LORD.

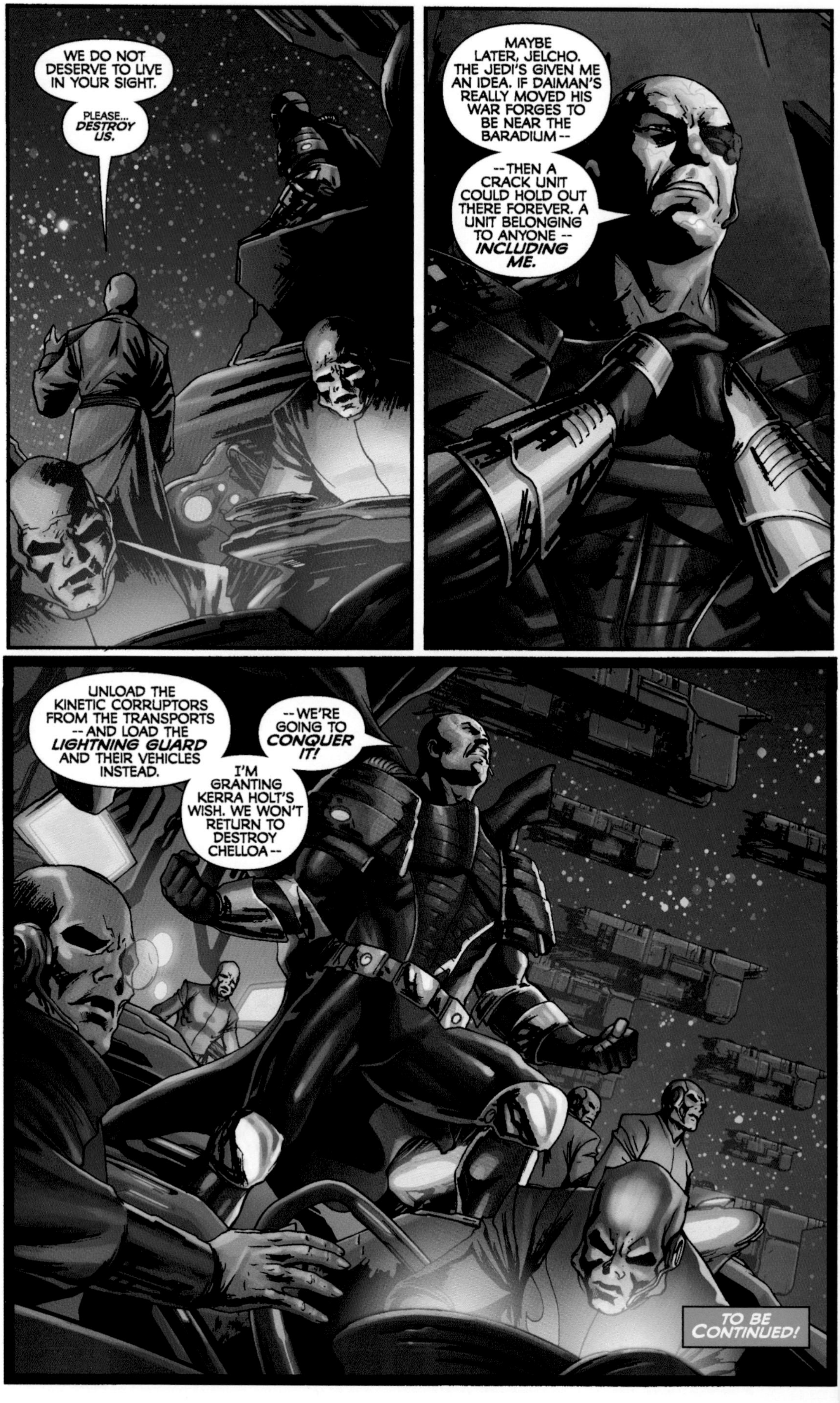
WE DO NOT DESERVE TO LIVE IN YOUR SIGHT.
PLEASE... DESTROY US.
MAYBE LATER, JELCHO. THE JEDI'S GIVEN ME AN IDEA. IF DAIMAN'S REALLY MOVED HIS WAR FORGES TO BE NEAR THE BARADIUM --
--THEN A CRACK UNIT COULD HOLD OUT THERE FOREVER. A UNIT BELONGING TO ANYONE -- INCLUDING ME.
UNLOAD THE KINETIC CORRUPTORS FROM THE TRANSPORTS -- AND LOAD THE LIGHTNING GUARD AND THEIR VEHICLES INSTEAD.
I'M GRANTING KERRA HOLT'S WISH. WE WON'T RETURN TO DESTROY CHELLOA --
--WE'RE GOING TO CONQUER IT!
TO BE CONTINUED!